Best of All

ILLUSTRATIONS BY SERGIO MARTINEZ

MAX LUCADO

SCHOLASTIC INC.
New York Toronto London Auckland Sydney
Mexico City New Delhi Hong Kong Buenos Aires

ISBN 0-439-64286-8

Published by Scholastic Inc., 557 Broadway, New York, NY 10012, by arrangement
with Crossway Books, a division of Good News Publishers. SCHOLASTIC and
associated logos are trademarks and/or registered trademarks of Scholastic Inc.

12 11 10 9 8 7 6 5   4 5 6 7 8 9/0

Printed in the U.S.A.   40

First Scholastic printing, January 2004

Design by UDG | Design Works, Sisters, Oregon   www.udgdesignworks.com

For Lane and Ebeth Dennis
With gratitude for your faith in God
and friendship with me.

"Higher on the right! Higher on the right!" demanded the mayor. There was no patience in his voice. Chip, the Wemmick lifting the banner, stretched as high as he could and pounded the nail into the pole.

"Better?" He'd barely asked the question when his ladder began to sway, first to one side, then the next. CRASH! Chip grabbed the nail he'd just hammered and held on.

"Perfect!" declared the mayor. "Just perfect!"

As Wemmicks ran to the rescue of the dangling worker, the mayor's wife read aloud the words stretched over the street: "Wemmicksville Welcomes Miss Bess Stovall."

"Oh!" She clapped her hands as she spoke. "What a wonderful day! Whoever would have thought that such a famous person would visit our village? You know what they say, don't you?"

Everyone leaned forward. "When it comes to Wemmicks, she's the best— the best of all."

Punchinello and Lucia were near enough to overhear her words. Like the rest of the townspeople, they were wooden Wemmicks made by Eli the Wemmick-maker. Unlike the rest of the village, they were puzzled. "Tell me again," Punchinello asked the mayor's wife, "why is she so famous?"

"Because everyone knows her."

"But why does everyone know her?"

"Because she's famous."

"But why is she coming to Wemmicksville?" Punch asked.

The mayor's wife rolled her eyes in disgust. "Haven't you heard? She's here to choose members for the Wonderful Wemmicks Club."

Punchinello nodded like he understood, but he really didn't. He looked at Lucia, and she looked at him, and both shrugged their shoulders. He was just about to ask another question when the Watch-Wemmick on top of the hill shouted, "She's here! She's here!"

Doors flew open. Stores emptied. Villagers rushed from all directions to the end of Main Street. Fathers lifted children to their shoulders, and short Wemmicks elbowed their way to the front of the crowd. There was much shouting and pointing and tiptoe-standing until a uniformed wooden soldier, looking very official and formal, appeared at the turn in the road. With scroll in hand and bugle hanging from his neck, he marched over the Wemmick River Bridge and stopped in front of the crowd. Staring straight ahead at no one, he stood stiffly until all had hushed. Opening the scroll, he read in a loud voice:

"Cut from the grandest forest, carved from the strongest tree,
Full of sap—only the purest—she's of the highest pedi-tree.
So welcome, ye Wemmicks, to your village so small,
The noblest grain from the finest lumber—
She is Bess Stovall!"

With snappy movements, he tucked the scroll under his arm and pulled the bugle to his lips. Bah-dah-dah-dah-dah-Bah!!! What the Wemmicks saw next caused a village-wide gasp. A squad of soldiers marched around the corner, shouldering a tall box with curtains. From behind him Punchinello heard the crowd whisper, "It's her!" The box sat on two poles, and the poles rested on the shoulders of four soldiers. Two guards walked in front. Two walked in back.

Boots on the wooden bridge made the only sound. Click, click, click. They kept in perfect step until one of the soldiers stumbled, just slightly. The box leaned out over the water. The villagers gasped a second time. Let the box lean much farther, and the guest of honor would fall into the fast-flowing river. But the soldiers straightened themselves, crossed the bridge, and came to a stop in front of the mayor and his wife. They lowered the box.

The trumpet-toting, scroll-reading servant stepped forward and, after a long pause, pulled back the curtain. As Bess stepped out, the villagers stepped back. They'd never seen a wooden person quite like Miss Bess Stovall.

Feathers flumed out of her hat. Earrings dangled to her shoulders. Both her lips and dress were bright red. Her shoes were tall, her nails were long, and, most noticeably, a large golden letter M hung from her neck.

When she snapped her fingers, a sentry handed her a white cloth. With it she carefully wiped the M and held it up like a mirror before her face. Seeing her reflection, she adjusted her hair and smiled. Bess Stovall was pleased with herself. With eyes peering down her high nose, she held out her hand, allowing it to fall forward at the wrist. "Ahem."

The mayor's wife understood the gesture. She elbowed her husband. "Kiss it." He did.

And when he did, the visitor spoke. "What good fortune is yours that I have come your way." She smirked, head back, hand still extended. The mayor's wife curtsied and motioned for the other Wemmicks to do the same. They did. Even the men.

"Shall we get on with the greetings?" Bess asked.

"Of course," answered the mayor. "Everyone in line."

One by one the citizens of Wemmicksville passed before their guest.

"Yes, yes," she would reply to whatever was said to her.

"Welcome to our village."

"Yes, yes."

"We're glad you're here."

"Yes, yes."

"We are honored."

"Yes, yes."

She was less concerned about what they said than what she saw. Occasionally she would pause and stare deeply at a Wemmick. She examined the nose of the storeowner and the ear of his son. She ran a gloved thumb across the hand of the house-builder and took a long look at the forehead of the painter.

No one knew what she was looking for, and no one asked. (Although the wife of the mayor acted as if she knew, nodding when the famous guest nodded and sighing when she sighed.) The shortest and longest looks were given to Punchinello and Lucia.

Upon seeing Punchinello, Bess suddenly stepped back before he could touch her hand. Lifting her nose and waving, she instructed, "Go on, go on." Stunned, Punch didn't move. He just stood there, curious.

"Move on," her servant repeated with a firm voice. Punchinello did.

Lucia started to follow him, not wanting the same treatment. Suddenly the grand visitor stopped Lucia. "My, my," Bess Stovall admired, "what have we here?" Her eyes widened, and for the very first time since she began greeting Wemmicks, a smile softened her narrow face. "Such fine grain and a nice shade. Are you maple?"

Lucia didn't understand. "Excuse me?"

"Are you made of maple?"

She had to think before answering. "Yes."

"Which forest?"

Lucia paused and thought. It took some time to remember. "Majestic," she finally answered.

Bess placed her hand over her mouth in surprise. "Then you and I are of the same family tree!"

"We are?"

Bess Stovall laughed. "Of course." She then leaned forward and whispered, "How nice to find someone of my roots. Stay around and we will talk."

Lucia did. Between greetings Bess Stovall would make remarks to Lucia beneath her breath such as, "Ugh, what knotty timber," or "Such an inferior grove," or "Definitely from the wrong side of the mountain." Lucia understood none of the comments, but she didn't say so.

After all the greetings, Bess signaled for Lucia to step near. "Tomorrow we must chat. I have something for you," she said, fingering her M necklace. With that she turned and left, escorted by the soldiers, followed by the mayor and his wife.

Punchinello approached Lucia. "Did I do something wrong?"

"I don't know."

"Did you do something right?"

"I don't know."

"Why is she kind to some Wemmicks and rude to others?"

"I think it has something to do with your ancest-tree."

"My what?"

"What forest you come from."

"Why does that matter?"

"I don't know."

They turned and left the village. Neither one spoke. They hadn't known they were different, and now that they did, they didn't know how to feel. "I'll see you tomorrow," Punch finally said.

"Yeah, sure," Lucia replied.

Neither felt too happy.

As the days passed, they saw each other less and less. It took Bess Stovall only a short time to select her favorite Wemmicks for the Wonderful Wemmicks Club. Lucia was among them. So were the storeowner and Mr. and Mrs. Mayor. Bess gave each an M to wear around the neck.

"The M is for maple. You are maples," she explained as she showed them how to polish the medallion. "Not all Wemmicks are equal. Some are common, made of pine or elm. A few are quality, cut from maple like you. Fewer still of us are from a fine family tree." She glanced at Lucia, and Lucia blushed. The other Wemmicks politely applauded.

"And then," Bess Stovall curled her lip as if she'd just tasted something sour, "some Wemmicks are willows."

"Willows?" they asked.

"Willow is weak wood," the maple Wemmick explained. "It bends. It bruises. Shallow roots. No one wants to be a willow."

"Do you know any?" the mayor's wife asked.

"Actually there's one in your village."

They all leaned forward, curious. Bess looked again at Lucia. "Your friend."

"Punchinello?" Lucia asked.

Everyone gasped. "I always knew he was weaker," someone said.

"Been suspecting a bad family for years," another agreed.

"Such a sapling," added a third. The rest nodded. Lucia nodded with them.

From that day forward Wemmicksville began to change. Townspeople took notice of each other's tree type. The walnuts looked down on the pines. The pines looked down on the elms. The maples looked down on everyone, and everyone looked down on Punchinello.

Walnuts formed a club and opened several branches. Elms cut a path and named it Elm Street. Maples built a tree house and hosted M-polishing parties. Everyone had a group. Everyone, that is, except Punchinello. Even Lucia ignored him.

"Hi, Lucia," he would say to her.

"Yes, yes," she would reply, not stopping. She was, after all, cut from the finest tree. And Punchinello was just a willow Wemmick—soft and easily bent.

One day Punchinello felt especially alone. He went to the Pine Picnic, but no one sat by him. The walnuts were playing games, but no one threw him the ball. He even tried to go to the maple party, but the sign on the door said, "Royal-tree Only."

Punchinello was very sad. He went for a walk and sat down by the river where the willow trees grew.

"Why did I have to be a willow?" he said aloud to no one.

"What would you rather have been?"

The sound of the voice startled Punchinello. He turned and saw Eli, his maker.

"Maple?" Eli continued. "Would you rather be made of maple?"

Punchinello didn't answer. Both sad and embarrassed, he lowered his head. Eli walked over and lifted Punch's chin with a finger.

"Other Wemmicks are better," Punchinello told him.

"Who says?"

"Everyone."

Eli sighed and shook his head. "Come here." The two walked over to a willow tree and stopped.

"Punchinello, who do you think knows more, the Wemmicks or the Wemmick-maker?"

Punchinello smiled softly. "The maker."

"Of course I do. Do you think I knew what I was doing when I made you?" The look in Eli's eyes convinced Punchinello that he was about to hear something important. "You are special, my child. You are the way you are because I made you that way."

"You chose my forest?"

"Yes."

"You chose my wood?"

"Yes."

"Willow is just as special as maple?"

"Just as special."

"Then why do the others treat me like I am not?"

"Here is someone you can ask."

"Hi, Punch." This time the voice was Lucia's. Punch turned. "I'm sorry," she said, "I've been listening too much to them and not enough to Eli."

Punchinello shrugged. He noticed that she wasn't wearing her M necklace. "That's okay."

Both smiled. "Want to go back to the village?" she asked. "Today is the big send-off for Bess Stovall."

"Yeah, I'd like that."

The two said good-bye to Eli and walked toward Wemmicksville. Many Wemmicks turned when they entered the village. More than one whispered and pointed as the maple Wemmick and the willow Wemmick walked side by side. But Punchinello and Lucia didn't care. They were glad to be friends again.

All of Wemmicksville turned out to say good-bye to Miss Bess Stovall. She stepped into her box and signaled that she was ready to go. Her soldier escorts marched proudly before her. Her bugler sounded the farewell. Wemmicks lined up on either side of the river to watch. New members of the Wonderful Wemmicks Club wore their club T-shirts with pride.

Crossing the bridge, the honored guest waved her gold medallion at the crowd. "Farewell, lowly Wemmicks. Perhaps someday I'll honor you again with my presence," she shouted.

Bess Stovall leaned out the window of her special box so that everyone could see her. As she did, she leaned a bit too far, and began falling, falling . . .

Her tumble stopped when her medallion chain caught on the bridge rail. When it snapped in half, she grabbed one end and held on, the river roaring beneath her.

Wemmicks cried with alarm. "Help her!" the mayor's wife shouted.

"Save her!" someone yelled.

"But no one can reach her," said an onlooker.

"I can't hold on much longer!" Bess shrieked.

Soldiers tried. Wemmicks tried. No success. They were too stiff to bend underneath the bridge.

"Let me try!" shouted Punchinello. "I'm made of limber lumber." Not waiting for an answer, he ran to the edge of the bridge and sat with his back to the river. "Grab my legs." When the soldiers did, he leaned back, bent over double, and twisted around until he was hanging upside down. Instantly, he could see the wide-eyed Wemmick. She was clinging to the chain, her feet pulled by the river.

"I'm coming," he shouted. Then to the amazement of everyone, he bent back, back, back until he was under the bridge reaching for the desperate Bess.

"Take my hand," he offered.

This time she didn't care what kind of wood she touched. She grabbed his hand and held on.

"You must let go of the chain," Punchinello instructed.

Bess Stovall obeyed the little Wemmick, letting go of her precious medallion and watching it fall into the river below.

Punchinello swung forward, pulling Bess high enough to be grabbed by the soldiers. Within moments Punchinello and Bess were safe on the bridge and surrounded by Wemmicks. "How did you do that?" everyone asked.

"It's easy when you're made of the right wood." He smiled.

For several moments no one spoke. Then from the back one of the maple Wemmicks walked up to Punch. He removed his M from its chain and turned it upside down, making a W. "Enough of all this talk about maples. Let's just be Wemmicks." Hanging the W around Punchinello's neck, he added, "Punchinello, you're the Wemmick of the day."

One by one the maple Wemmicks removed their M's, placing them on the ground near Punchinello. Soon there was a small pile of medallions. Even the mayor and his wife removed theirs, though she took one last look at herself in her M before she set it down.

The Wemmicks started back toward town.
The last thing anyone could remember about Miss
Bess Stovall was seeing the majestic maple down by
the river, searching all alone for her precious gold
medallion.

As for the villagers, they quit talking about
ancest-trees and decided to just be Wemmicks again.
And Punchinello? He had a new job in town.
"Say, Punch," a new Wemmick friend asked on the
way back to the village, "there's a ball stuck in my
chimney. Any chance you could reach it?"

And when Punch did, he looked up the hill.
Eli was watching from the porch of his house.
Punch waved. His maker smiled.